LOST VOICE IN A FOREIGN LAND

A NOVEL

ADEWUNMI O. ANIFOWOSHE

SYNOPSIS

This is a fictional story of a Nigerian lady coming to the UK for the first time in search of greener pasture only to face a major roadblock to fully live and enjoy her freedom. She leaves Nigeria hoping to attain high educational qualifications, sending regular money back home to make her family live a better life, and raising a family.

Her first step on the land feels so refreshing, but as the days go by, things get blurry and bleak. However, with faith and endurance, the light in the tunnel becomes brighter and brighter.

DEDICATION

I dedicate this book to everyone caught up in the systems of a foreign land.

To everyone who has left their country of origin for foreign soil with the hope of achieving more than they could back at home, only to face stiff restrictions caused by their inability to possess necessary documents or to fit into the system.

To everyone who finds themselves in the land of greener pastures, thought to be flowing with milk and honey, but yet to reap from its abundance.

To everyone living in plenty yet empty, I encourage you to keep up the faith.

Soon, you shall regain your voice and get to the top. Failure is not on the ladder of success, so never look down. Keep looking forward and upward; in no time, you will find water in the dry well. You will eventually find your voice.

The LORD *will fight for you, and you shall hold[a] your peace." Exodus 14:14*

New King James Version

Chapter One

The news of moving from one's country of residence to richer and greener pastures is usually the best news most people in developing countries desire to hear. As a result, when you hear anyone say, I'm traveling out, you may not need to ask as you already expect the destination to either be Europe, the USA, or mostly the UK. You have mixed feelings about whether to 'celebrate' with the person or to be jealous of them. To top it all, the thought of Wow! I seem to be the only one left in this country fills up your head.

There are folks, however, who do not think traveling out is worth the hype; and are satisfied with going on periodic vacations and coming back to one's home country. But traveling out is often synonymous with the feeling of freedom, like a bird let out a cage with the chance to fly wherever it wishes, especially from a country like Nigeria. So when Eva got a call from her Auntie Tonia that she would take her to the UK, that her passport was already sorted and all she needed to do was to pack her suitcase, she could barely contain the joy and excitement and she ran off telling her friends how much she would miss them already. She promised to keep in touch with them and offer help if they ever wanted to also come over.

Phew! After years of finishing high school with no funds to further my education, this news is nothing but prayers answered.

Auntie Tonia had told her she would attend a College, after which she would proceed to the university.

She was immediately lost in thoughts and daydreamed of how she would get to the UK, start College, get a good job, and start making money. She was too sure of a better life ahead of her and she excitedly promised her parents to send money to them every month once she got paid.

She thought of all the good things she had heard and watched about the UK, the constant power supply, the fancy clothes, people sending money, cars, and other amazing stuff back home to their family in Nigeria.

She imagined herself in her mansion, driving the best car, wearing lovely clothes, effortlessly making lots of money. She got so preoccupied with her thoughts so much that sleep eluded her at night. She was wide awake, counting down to the departure date.

She had done a good job with her imagination that even when she eventually fell asleep, all her dreams were nothing short of living the good life in the UK. She planned to use the few days before her flight to perfect her hair-making skills because she had been told that she could make extra money with that.

On the day of her departure, with tears in her eyes, she hugged her parents and siblings goodbye. It was a tough moment for her as she had never been that far from them before. However, she said her goodbyes with great hopes and expectation that a better future awaited her.

Her first challenge started at the immigration area of the airport. The officer felt something was not right with her passport. Thankfully, she didn't have to deal much with that as her auntie and her husband were on ground to help resolve the issue and before long they were allowed to proceed with the checks.

Throughout the journey, you could tell she was beside herself with excitement. She kept smiling and saying thank you to her auntie and uncle. The flight felt so long, but she was calm and enjoyed every bit of it.

After a few hours of staying wide awake with excitement, she was finally drifting off to sleep when her uncle tapped her.

"Eva, when we get to the UK airport, make sure you don't say a word. Allow us to do the talking."

Eva nodded, "Ok, Uncle."

Eva wondered why. She cared little anyway. She was ready to do whatever was necessary to get to the UK, the land flowing with milk & honey as popularly called by the people back home.

Sleep had now left her eyes, so she adjusted her seat. She finished the light meal served on the flight with so much contentment. She was on her way to the UK after all and would soon have the best of meals. Fortunately, she had landed a seat by the window, so she had the lovely cloudy view for company. Her thoughts of the UK were getting more and more concretized.

About thirty minutes to the end of the flight, the hostess' voice was heard giving information on what to do as the plane prepared to land. She fastened her belt and put on her hat, which she had taken off whilst on the plane.

Auntie Tonia and her husband had asked her to wear the hat and, without asking questions, she complied. She thought, *that must be how they dress in the UK*. She has always loved wearing a hat back at home anyway, so it was a good thing she had loads of it. One of her friends had told her people wore a lot of hats because of the weather there, so they were one of the first sets of clothing she packed.

The plane eventually got to a still after running on the tarmac for nearly three minutes. Activity resumed in the plane as passengers made to pick their hand luggage. Eva got hers and walked close to her auntie and uncle as they joined the queue toward the conveyor belt to collect the rest of the luggage. They got their items of luggage and moved toward the Customs & Immigration.

Eva noticed Auntie Tonia and her husband were unusually quiet, so she also decided to be quiet. She's normally called a chatterbox by her friends, and the excitement that came with this trip added to it. If she talks, she would explode with ecstasy, hence she ensured she stayed quiet. She wanted to ask if everything was okay, but wasn't sure that would be a good move.

They had told her to be quiet, so she had better stay quiet. As they successfully scaled through the Customs & Immigration checkpoint, she noticed a change in their countenance. Auntie Tonia and her husband's attitude changed, and they now looked relieved and happy. She didn't understand why and asked her auntie what happened. Auntie Tonia promised to tell her when they got home.

As Eva sat on her uncle's car *"which was parked in the airport"*, she found the view fascinating. It was a vast difference from what she knew in Nigeria. The street lights shone so brightly it looked like it was still the thick of the day, though it was twenty-five minutes past eight o'clock in the evening already. Motorists enjoyed a smooth ride with no halt caused by bumps from possible bad roads, as was the norm in Nigeria.

Soon they arrived at a beautifully furnished apartment in a warm neighborhood and were welcomed by two little children, a boy and a girl. They were her auntie's children. They were excited to see their parents but surprised to see Eva.

They did not know who she was, so they had a face full of questions. They greeted her in the Nigerian way.

"Hello, auntie."

Though they lived in the UK, they were used to greeting this way. In the Nigerian culture, an older person could be called an auntie or uncle, whether they were related to you or not. Eva replied the greeting with a 'hello,' keenly observing them. This was her first time meeting her nephew and niece.

They helped her with the little bags while asking their mum if she brought back any goodies from Nigeria, amongst a million other questions. A lady came out to welcome them and Eva presumed she was their nanny, especially with the way she came running. As the lady helped with the luggage, Eva stole glances around the apartment. It was love at first sight.

The nanny asked to take Eva to her room. While they walked to Eva's new room, she got to find out the nanny was from Nigeria as well and has been in the UK for the past ten years. The room was big, beautiful, and also very spacious. Eva could not take it all in.

"Thank you, God," she exclaimed in a gasp.

The nanny smiled, "Auntie, you're welcome"

"Please ma, don't call me auntie. My name is Eva." Eva cut her politely.

"Okay. And my name is Bose."

"It's good to meet you, Sister Bose."

"Dinner will be ready in few minutes. Let me leave you to relax, have a change of clothes, and come down to eat." Sister Bose told her.

"Thank you."

After their meal, Eva was already sleepy. She asked her auntie if she could speak with her parents to let them know they had arrived safely before going to bed. Her auntie called them via her phone. She had a few minutes with them, bade them goodnight, and went off to bed. She slept like a baby.

Chapter Two

Eva woke up rather early the next morning. She sat up looking out of the window, wondering how everywhere was bright yet silent, as against the hustle and bustle of Lagos that woke you up as early as 4 am. A knock on her door startled her. She went to open the door. It was Sister Bose, the nanny.

"Good morning and how was your night?" Sister Bose asked.

"It was nice, but I woke up early," Eva replied.

She would need some more nights to get adjusted to her new room and the environment.

"Would you like to see around the house? I can take you on a tour when you're ready."

"Oh, thank you! I'll like that right away."

Eva straightened her pyjama, put on her slippers, and followed her excitedly like a kid off to a candy store. First, sister Bose showed her the kitchen, then the garden. Eva was so happy to see the big, beautiful garden. She imagined sitting out there reading a book or doing some writing.

"Sister Bose, why is the entire area so quiet with no one on the street?" Eva asked.

Sister Bose laughed as she explained to her that most places in the UK are quiet and people do not start their day like a troop, as is the practice in Nigeria.

"People go to work at different hours of the day, which makes it a less noisy situation."

After some minutes of chatting and answering Eve's questions, Sister Bose told her she would have to go back inside, as she needed to make breakfast.

Eva offered to help her in the kitchen.

Eva thought this was a good time to get to know Sister Bose better. She wondered why a grown woman would decide to be a house help and nanny in the UK. As Sister Bose prepared the breakfast, Eva seized the opportunity to ask Sister Bose all the questions running in her mind.

"Sister Bose, when did you come to the UK?" Eva asked.

"I've been in the UK for the past ten years."

Eva was shocked.

"Really? How long have you been working for my auntie?"

Sister Bose laughed.

"Ermmm… I have been working for them for the past ten years. Your auntie came to pick me from Nigeria to help take care of her child, the firstborn who is now ten years old. I met your auntie for the first time where I used to help them sell food in Idumota. After a while, we lost touch, and I didn't see her again. A year after, she contacted me and asked if I could travel to the UK with her for work. That was one of the best days of my life. I cried so hard as I never thought I would ever have the opportunity to travel out of Nigeria. I quickly said yes."

"I was a single mother of two then, though my children were living with my mum in the village at the time. I knew if I travelled to the UK I can send money to help them and give them a better life. I quickly called my mother to tell her and she gave me her blessings. That is how I came to the UK and I have been working for your auntie since then." Sister Bose wrapped up her narration.

Eva knew she was asking too many questions, but she shrugged that thought off after all her nickname back in Nigeria was 'Madam too much question'. She enjoyed asking questions and talked a lot too.

"So why didn't you go to school then?"

"How can I do that while taking care of Tobi. It was a full-time job. Two years after, Dumininu was born so taking care of both children was hard work."

"I decided to start sewing on my free days. Your auntie bought me a machine, and she introduced some of her friends to me. With the money I get from sewing alongside my salary, I have been able to send my children to a better school. I also rented a better apartment for my mum. They are living a better life and I am satisfied with that. I don't miss not going to school as I derive my joy from their happiness."

Eva was surprised at how content sister Bose sounded. She already felt more like a part of her auntie's family than a house help. Eva was still curious, so she continued her round of questioning.

"So what happened to your children's father?"

Sister Bose sighs, "Hmmm... He's somewhere in Nigeria. He left me after the second child and went with a lady who he had been lying to me was his sister; only for me to find them together in bed. The last time I saw him was when my second child clocked one year. She is thirteen years now."

"I thank God for everything. When he left, I thought my life would end. Thank God for my mother. She was my rock. She stood solidly behind me and cared for me and my children until a friend asked me to come to Lagos from the village to work with her for a better life. You see what God has done for me. He sent me helpers every step of my life."

"Sister Bose, are you seeing anyone at the moment?"

Sister Bose's face flushed as she smiled.

"There is one man that has been disturbing me for a relationship, but I have not said yes for now. I am most concerned about my children and would not want any man to mistreat me. But I know that when the time is right, I will find the right one."

Sister Bose continued, "One has to be careful with men, especially Nigerian men in the UK. Most of them are liars who just want to sleep with you and dump you. Don't get me wrong. There are decent ones, but you have to choose the right one prayerfully. Not everyone is like your uncle. He's a good and godly man too."

Sister Bose then asked Eva, "What about you? Do you have a boyfriend?"

Eva replied, "No, I have always had admirers, but I'm not ready. I always prayed that when the right one comes, God will tell me. But for now, I just want to face my studies and achieve all I have always dreamt of."

Breakfast was now ready and they could hear the footsteps of other family members in the house. The kitchen door opened, and Tobi ran to hug Sister Bose and greeted her. Dumininu followed closely too. You could tell that the children loved her.

Chapter Three

As they put the food on the table, Eva could tell how much Tobi and Dumininu were fond of Sister Bose. Sister Bose seemed to be fulfilling destiny by staying with this family. Eva felt at peace to be here.

Later in the day, Auntie Tonia would take her and the children on a visit to Auntie Nike's family, a family friend they all knew from Nigeria. Auntie Nike's daughter was a student at the college Eva would be attending, so her auntie wanted them to meet so Eva could get some information on school registration and general college life.

Breakfast went on in silence. After eating, Sister Bose helped the children get ready for the trip. Eva went back to her room to have a bath and get dressed. She put on some makeup too. Her heart was exploding with delight at the thought of seeing the city. She was excited to finally see Auntie Nike after a long time and her children for the first time.

They set out in Uncle's jeep. Eva had her eyes out the window nearly the entire ride as she marvelled at the beauty of the city. The children were busy with their tablets, so it gave her ample time to take in all the sights with no distractions from them.

As they drove by a bridge, Auntie Tonia called Eva's attention.

"That's the famous London Bridge always talked about in Nigeria."

Eva took a long look at the bridge, trying to connect what she saw with what she already knew about it. She looked forward to doing a proper tour of the city while taking lovely pictures to send to her family and friends back at home.

After a 30 minute drive, they arrived at Auntie Nike's house. A lady, Eva assumed to be Auntie Nike's daughter, received them at the door.

"Hello. You're welcome. My mum will be with you shortly."

Eva stole a glance around the well-arranged and decorated living room. She caught a family portrait of Auntie Nike with her two girls and a boy. In her head, she tried to guess which of the girls in the photo it was she would attend college with.

Auntie Nike walked in while Eva was lost in her thoughts.

"Wow! You have grown so much since the last time I saw you." Auntie Nike exclaimed.

"I think you were about fifteen years then, but look at you now, all grown into a lady. It's so good to see you."

Auntie Nike wrapped her in a welcoming embrace.

"Your auntie said you will attend the same school with Sophie, my daughter."

She called Sophie to come and meet Eva.

Sophie was the lady who welcomed them at the door. She looked like she was in her 20s or maybe they were age mates. Eva felt they would get along well.

"You're welcome to the UK. I hope you'll enjoy your stay here," Sophie said to her warmly.

Eva noticed her British accent, but she could still make out her words.

"Thank you so much."

Auntie Nike asked if they would like to eat as she has made a very delicious *Efo riro* (Spinach) and some assorted meat stew for them. Eva's auntie said they would eat later as they just had their breakfast recently.

Sophie brought in some snacks and drinks. By this time, the children had disappeared into one of the rooms. You could tell they were familiar with the house. Sophie and Eva went off to Sophie's room for their little chitchat too. As they walked away, Eva overheard Auntie Nike ask her auntie if she had got her a job yet. For some seconds, Eva shuddered at the thought of having to work while schooling. She brushed it off. *I could do a lot with the money, anyway.*

They walked past the children in another sitting room with a boy Eva assumed to be Sophie's brother, the same one in the picture. He said 'hello' to her as they passed. Sophie's closets had all sorts of fancy clothing.

Eva admired the array of brightly coloured clothes, nice shoes, trainers, and bags. She smiled to herself. *This would be me in a few months.*

Sophie pointed to a chair for Eva to sit on while she sat on her bed. Eva could feel her inquisitive spirit kicking in and the thousands of questions running riot in her mind, waiting to be let loose. She fought to stifle the urge to ask Eva any question, but it was an attempt in futility as the question literally dropped from her mouth.

"Sophie, were you born here?"

Slightly taken aback by the question, she turned to Eva and managed a smile.

"Yes, I was and have never left since I was born."

Eva thought there was no point holding back, so she let the questions flow.

"So how does it feel living in the UK?"

Sophie smiled, "I can't tell the difference since I have lived nowhere else, but from what mum tells me and the stories I hear, I think I would rather stay here than live in Nigeria. The power supply is steady, there is a regular supply of water, the streets are clean and better, so I think life in the UK is better. I would still love to pay a visit to Nigeria though."

They had some more small talk about life in the UK.

"I'm pretty excited to start my registrations at the College on Monday. Can you fill me in on some information I need to know?"

"It is a nice college. There are lots of Nigerian students, which is one of the reasons I went there. My classes are three days a week, Mondays, Wednesdays, and Fridays. Yours might be different. You would know better when you get your enrolment done on Monday."

"What course are you enrolling for, by the way?"

"I'm not sure, but I think my auntie once mentioned I'll be studying Health Science."

Sophie screamed with enthusiasm.

"Wow, that's exactly what I am studying. I intend to study Nursing in the University after College."

"Do you work too?" Eva asked.

"Yes, I work two days when I am not in college and sometimes on weekends," Sophie replied.

"What do you do?"

"I work as a Carer in a Residential home and sometimes as an Agency Nursing Assistant (NA) at the hospital."

"What is a Residential home?" Eva looked puzzled.

"It is an old people's home. Some old people are not sick but just need a place where they can be helped and taken care of."

"Is it a tough job to do?" Eva wondered.

"No. I enjoy doing it. I see it as a progressive step to my nursing career."

Eva feels skeptical about the job. She didn't think she will cope with it. She always loved challenges anyway, so she was ready to take this on and do well at it too. This was the job Auntie Tonia would most likely get her, so she would have to put her best foot forward.

"There is a current vacancy at my place of work. I can take you there and they could offer you the job. All you need to do is to shadow someone who would teach you the ropes. I could also volunteer to put you through the basics of what we do." Sophie explained to her like she knew the exact thoughts in Eva's head at the time.

Eva felt so relieved. She sensed a renewed courage to take on this journey ahead of her with Sophie as her friend and guardian angel. *Maybe it won't be as tough as I thought after all.*

"Thank you so much, Sophie."

"It's my pleasure," Eva smiled.

Sophie sensed the bout of questions was over, so she brought out her coursework and showed Eva just to prepare her for Monday. They were on the second page when Auntie Nike's voice rang through the corridor.

"It's time to eat."

Chapter Four

Sunday mornings in Nigeria always started at 5 am. Breakfast was not a thing back at home, but Eva's mum always ensured the Sunday meal was prepared, so they do not have to do any cooking when they come back from church. Her dad played his regular Sunday music while getting ready for church. Everyone was out of the house by 7 am as church started at 8 am.

The routine was different here. Her auntie had told her their church would start at noon, which Eva interpreted to be an afternoon service. Though she woke up at 6 am, she didn't feel well-rested enough. She was not sure what to do with the time ahead of her, especially as service was still a couple of hours later.

She spent the first hours lazing around, then she read through her bible, hoping that by 10 am she would have her bath and get dressed for church. She looked forward to the service, eager to see the way they did church service here.

Her auntie also told her they would go out for a meal after service. The day looked exciting already.

"Eva!!!"

Her auntie's voice woke her from sleep. She had fallen asleep while reading. She had been sleeping for a few hours.

"Get ready. We are leaving by 11 am."

Eva doubled her pace and by 10.45 am she was ready. She went downstairs to join the rest of the family having breakfast already.

"Would you like to have some breakfast?" Sister Bose asked her.

"No, thank you," came her reply.

She was not used to eating before church. Back at home, they always fasted until they returned from church.

It was a 30-minute drive to the church. They arrived just in time for the start of service. Eva was a tad amazed at the promptness of time. *Why did we have to leave exactly 30 minutes before the start of service? What if they got stuck in traffic?* Church back in Nigeria was a 15-minute drive from home, but they had to leave an hour before the service. The journey to church here was too smooth compared to what she was familiar with. They were in the church at exactly 30minutes. They joined the Sunday School, which lasted another 30 minutes before the actual service began.

Eva enjoyed the entire service but missed the loud clapping and dancing that characterised praise and worship back home. Aside from that, she loved all other parts of the service, including the sermon. The newcomers were specially welcomed by taking them to a lovely room where they were served snacks, drinks, and a gift.

After service, they had lunch at a Chinese buffet restaurant. The spread of food before Eva overwhelmed her.

"You can have as much food as you want."

She loved food, but she was not a big eater.

Sis Bose offered to take her around the buffet with the children so she could see the choices available. The children went straight for chips, but sister Bose told Eva to go for the starters first and to go easy on the starters, so as not to get full on it before the main course and dessert.

"Hmm. Nice suggestion. How much can I eat, though?" she asked.

"Take your time. We have enough time to spend here."

They chatted while eating, sharing their unique experiences of their first visit to the UK. Her uncle recounted his experience in a buffet restaurant.

"I ate so much that I could not walk back to the car. It was so embarrassing I decided never to overeat again."

Tobi and Dumininu had a long laugh at their father's narration.

Three hours after and it didn't feel like it. They had so much fun.

"It's time to go…" Eva's auntie finally called out.

"Mum, one more ice cream please?" the children asked.

"Ok. Get on with that fast so we can take our leave please."

They asked Eva to go with them this time. She felt like they were getting used to her. She was happy.

Chapter Five

The week went by so quickly. Eva spent most of the time indoors. Her auntie said she needed the week to rest before the busy week started. After dinner one night, Eva sat down with the family to watch TV. She could barely concentrate, though. She rather relished in the thoughts that she was finally in the UK, something she never imagined possible. As they watched, her auntie called her to the kitchen to speak with her.

"Eva, remember I told you I will apply for a job for you. So you should get ready to take on the demands of work and your studies. I will introduce you to some of my friends who have Care Homes with vacancies. They will train you on the job, you'll need to learn fast."

This was exactly what Sophie had told her.

"That's fine, auntie. I don't mind resuming work now. But how will I find my way to and fro work since I am new?"

Auntie smiled.

"Of course, I won't leave you all by yourself. I will take you there and bring you back for the first few weeks till you make friends who can guide you. That will be all for now. If there's any more information you need to know, I'll tell you by morning tomorrow."

The next morning, Eva woke up to a knock on her door. It was 10 am. She never wakes up this late. She must have been so tired. She hurriedly got up to answer her door. It was auntie Tonia who was already dressed to go out.

"Good morning, Eva. Sorry to wake you up."

"No, aunty, it's fine. I always wake up at 7 am. I must have been exhausted last night."

"Okay. I needed to talk to you before leaving for work. There is something I didn't mention to you before we left Nigeria. When we applied for your visa, we had to do it through a College here so we could only apply for a 6-month duration, and we were told by the College that they will help renew it once you are here. This was part of the reasons we asked you not to talk at the airport if you remember. We didn't want you to answer questions wrongly. Thankfully, you were not asked questions at all."

She continued, "We had to tell them you were only spending three weeks and with the type of visa you have, you can only go to college and work for only 16hrs a week, which is not a lot. So we have asked one of our friends to give you a full-time job, but unfortunately, it's not legal. However, if you have to make money, that's the only way we can do it."

"My advice is that you should be careful and not talk about your status here to anyone because you don't know who to trust. I will take you to where you will work tomorrow."

Eva was further coached on how to do the job she was to start the next day. Everything sounded odd, new, and scary to her, but going back to Nigeria was not an option anymore.

Right there and then, she knew her voice had been stolen from her. She has just been told to be cautious of her surroundings, be vigilant of everyone that approaches or tries to be too close to her. She had to be sceptical of who she spoke with or made friends with. *Is this the way life is in the UK?*

She felt different emotions as she walked her auntie to the sitting room. She was afraid but also looked forward to making money. In all, she was grateful that her auntie took the risk to bring her to the UK, and right there she made a promise in her heart not to betray Auntie Tonia and her husband or get them into trouble.

After her auntie left, Eva lay in bed thinking of what the future held for her, starting from tomorrow. She had heard stories of people who have been in the UK for years and cannot go back to Nigeria, but she never knew it would happen to her. Sleep soon caught up with her. She saw herself in a group of white people. They requested to know her culture and nationality. They wanted to know what she had come to the UK for. She was about to answer their questions when Auntie Tonia's voice rang loudly in her head. *Don't talk to anybody. Don't trust anybody. Don't form a friendship with anyone.* In her aunt's voice mixed with hers, she responded, 'No, I can't do this' and she jumped up only to realise she had been dreaming.

The next day, rubbing her eyes as the early sun shone through her window. She checked the time. It was 5 am. Her auntie had told her they needed to leave home at 8 am. She listened for any voice from other parts of the house, but heard none. She looked out the window. *How can a place look so bright and promising yet fill one with so much fear of losing one's identity and voice?*

She had her bath and chose a bright dress. That should help to brighten her mood at least and boost her mood for the task ahead.

"Are you set, Eva?" Auntie Tonia asked from the hallway as she approached her room.

"Yes, auntie."

"We will set out at 8 am."

The meeting for the job went well. Eva was told to start on Monday. She will also enroll at the College on Monday. Eva applied for a one year course and after 6months she will need to re-register to renew her visa of 6months.

Eva was happy to start school and to make new friends. She looked forward to spending time with Sophie, who also attended the same college. She spent the rest of her day looking out her room window, fantasizing about this new life at school she was starting.

Chapter Six

It's Monday, the day Eva would start College. It was a new phase ahead of her. Though tensed, she was excited for the opportunity. Sophie would be there, so she had no fear of being alone. They were to leave home at 8 am. Her auntie would go with her. She was ready at 7 am with all her documents packed and tucked in a lovely bag her auntie gave her to use as a College bag. Sister Bose had breakfast ready downstairs while waiting for her auntie, Eva and the children had their breakfast.

She now knew her way around the house. The children were also ready for school. Her auntie would drop them off at school before taking her to College.

"Auntie Eva, are you accompanying mummy to drop us in school?"

"Yes," she answered them.

They smiled. "Good. You will get to know our school. Maybe one day, you will come and pick us from school too."

Eva replied, "I would love that."

"Are you all ready?" Her auntie asked as she met them downstairs at the dining area.

"Yessss," they chorused.

"Alright, let's get into the car."

Sister Bose brought the children's lunch bag and gave each of them theirs, while auntie gave Eva £10 to hold with her in case she needed to get a taxi home herself or to buy lunch. She made a mental note to ask Sophie to give Eva a ride home.

Eva was surprised as she didn't know Sophie drove. *That sounds fun.* First, she had a family who loves her and is accommodating, and then she was in college already, next she got a job offer, and now a friend who drives.

As they approached the children's school, the children tugged at Eva's clothes.

"Auntie Eva, that's our school. Can you come down with mummy to meet our friends?" Eva looked at her auntie and she nodded it was okay.

Tobi got down immediately they were in the parking lot.

"Come and meet my new auntie from Nigeria," he called one of his friends he had sighted nearby.

"Hello," Tobi's friend said with a smile in his voice.

Eva waved back, "Hello."

They walked Tobi to his class, as Auntie Tonia always did.

"Hello Miss. Meet my new auntie from Nigeria. Her name is auntie Eva"

"Hello, Auntie Eva! I hope you're enjoying your stay here."

"Yes, ma'am. Thank you."

She briskly waved goodbye before the teacher got a chance to ask another question.

They walked Dumininu to her class. She wasn't much of a talker like her brother, Tobi, but she was as excited to have Eva in her school. She also beckoned to one of her friends who was with her dad. Her friend's dad came over to greet auntie Tonia while Dumininu introduced Eva to her friend.

Dumininu and her friend were already holding hands and walking toward their class. At the class Dumininu and her friends hang their bags on their named hanger. Dumininu came to hug her mum and Eva.

"Bye, Dumininu. I will see you later." Says Eva

They began their drive to the College. Eva was excited yet tense about her first day.

"How do I find my way back home, auntie?" she asked.

"That's not a problem. Sophie can always give you a ride home; and on the days she can't, I'll tell her to show you where to get the bus."

"I'll also help you get your monthly bus pass soon," Auntie Tonia added.

"Thank you, Auntie."

After some more 10 minute drive, they arrived at the College. There was so much activity around her. The movement of students going about the premises made Eva feel a little shaky. She felt a little tug at her heart. *How will I fit in?* She quickly dismissed the thought. She was sure it won't be difficult to make friends. She had Sophie already too.

As they drove in, it was by a streak of coincidence that Eva saw Sophie just parking her car. She felt a sudden relief, as she wouldn't have to walk in alone. Sophie spotted them and she came to say hello to her auntie.

"Sophie, please can you show Eva the bus stop where to get a bus home? I will try to pick her up after college except you won't mind dropping her today."

"That's ok. I don't mind dropping her," Sophie said. "But on days I can't, I will tell her where to get the bus."

Auntie Tonia said goodbye and left. Eva and Sophie went to the registrar's office to enroll Eva and get her ID card. The process would take a few hours. Sophie had to leave Eva at the office for her class.

"I will meet you at the student lounge which I showed you earlier on."

They had gone on a quick tour when the registration queue was still very long.

Eva eventually completed her registration and went to wait for Sophie at the student lounge, as they had agreed.

"Hello?"

A voice distracted her. She turned to meet the face of an unfamiliar guy.

"Hello," she replied.

He had quite a warm personality, and soon they were chatting. She asked so many questions as they both walked towards the student lounge. From their chitchat, she gathered he has been a student in the college for 6 months, he is Ghanaian and plans to further study Medicine in a university outside London.

Sophie was waiting in the lounge when Eva and her new friend got there. Eva didn't know they had stood outside talking for that long. Sophie was surprised to see her chatting with a stranger, but she maintained a straight face. Eva introduced her new friend to Sophie and after a few more conversations, Sophie said they needed to leave and bade him goodbye.

On their way home, Sophie asked Eva about her new friend.

"Some guys prey on new students and take advantage of them. You'll need to be wary of them," Sophie advised.

"It's nothing to worry about. I don't intend to have a boyfriend, but thanks a lot for the heads up. I'll be careful."

They spent the remaining minutes' drive home catching up on the day's activities.

Sophie dropped Eva off at her home.

"See you on Wednesday!"

Her auntie was home. She was curious to know how Eva's first day at college went. Eva excitedly told her all about it. She looked forward to Wednesday and the rest of her stay in College.

The next 4months went well. Eva made more friends and got to know London well. Work was going on fine, though she sometimes got exhausted from her tight schedule. She has also travelled to another city outside of London with the family where she made more friends as well. Eva looked into universities she would like to go to after college.

Her Ghanaian friend, Michael, was becoming rather close. He wanted more than a friendship and Eva had to think if she was ready for a serious relationship yet. She was still new in the UK and Sophie had warned her against preying guys. She had to be careful.

They were spending more time together. He was a newbie, just like her. Though born in the UK, at age six his parents got a wonderful job offer in Ghana and they had to move there. He was only back in the UK to study. He always come for holiday every summer and stays with his grandmother who lives here. After college, he intends to proceed to the University of Scotland to study Medicine.

Eva was comfortable being just friends with him for now. She had things going well for her. She also had new friends in her church, which she appreciates.

Chapter Seven

After 6 months of study, it was exam day at the college. This exam would determine if she would get a chance to proceed to the university after College, the thought of that made her tense. As she got off the bus, she saw Michael, her Ghanaian friend. They both walked to the College as was their daily practice. They always met at the bus stop, same time, every college day.

Today all they talked about was the exam, how they looked forward to it and hoped to pass. The result would also determine the course Eva would study at the university. Michael was sure of himself, and he was certain he would pass. The vibes from both of them were positive and with that they walked into the college, parting ways as they got to the entrance of the study building.

Eva was so happy as the exam was what she expected. She and Sophie had planned to have lunch with Michael and Sophie's boyfriend, Richard, immediately after the exam. She got her stuff and went in search of Sophie so they could walk down to the restaurant for their lunch.

Sophie was waiting outside the classroom when Eva came out. It had been a long week studying for the exams and she was so excited to be finally done with it. To Eva, it was worth celebrating. Sophie looked a bit upset and distant. Eva noticed it and tried to find out what was going on but Sophie didn't seem willing to share what was on her mind, so Eva knew she had to let her be.

They walked silently to the restaurant where Michael and Sophie's boyfriend were waiting. As they walked in, Michael signalled for them to come over. When they were within earshot, Michael dropped a question that was related to why Sophie was quiet and distant. She looked at Sophie, back at Michael, then at Sophie's boyfriend who looked like he didn't know what Michael and Sophie were talking about.

At that point and at the same time, Richard and Eva asked, "What is it?"

Michael looked at Sophie, "So you heard about it too?"

Sophie nodded.

Eva and Richard waited for one of them to at least tell them what was going on.

"We heard the government is investigating the college and if found guilty, it may be closed down," Sophie said.

Eva was both shocked and surprised.

"How then would that affect us as students?" Eva was eager to know more.

"It means all students will have to move to another college, which may be a tough search, especially as it's the middle of the semester. It will be hard to find sufficient colleges to fit all the students in. Also, this is not good news for international students who need to renew their visas soon." Sophie attempted a detailed explanation.

At that instant, it dawned on Eva what this meant to her and she immediately got lost in thought. She remembered the conversation she had with her auntie a few days ago. Her visa was eligible for renewal soon and if she performed well in the just concluded exams, she stood a higher chance of getting her visa renewed. This was why she was pleased with the way the exam turned out. Now, this. *What will happen to my visa renewal? Will this mean I have to leave the UK?*

Several questions were begging for answers in her mind. All she wanted to do was to rush back home and have the discussion with her auntie. She had to keep calm though so that her friends at lunch would not assume there was any problem. Her mind flashes back to what her auntie had told her the previous months. *Do not trust anyone. Do not tell anyone about your status.* The past 6months thereabout had been a pretty smooth ride for her. She never thought these worries commonly faced by immigrants would eventually be her lot.

Though engrossed in her thoughts, she followed the discussion around the table. No one seemed to have noticed her reaction to the news. She was also not willing to talk about it if asked.

"This will be hard for international students as this means some of them won't be able to renew their visa and may be sent back or some would resort to living without legal papers. I have friends who have been in the UK for 10 years without papers to study or do a highly skilled job, so they had to settle for manual jobs. I know a guy who had a well-paying job back in Nigeria but came to the UK because of the lack of basic amenities back at home. He arrived here only to live a life he never envisaged. It is not a life I will like for people and it's worse if you have a friend in such a situation and cannot offer help."

That was Richard's voice.

Michael shared a contrary thought.

"I understand what you are saying and I have heard students talk about the fraudulent activities the College has been involved in. The College aids the immigration of people into the country for 'study' oblivious to them they were being investigated by the government. The College also charges the students exorbitant fees with the promise that they would help them renew their visas. Unfortunately, some of these people are not students but individuals who seize the opportunity to get into the UK and on their arrival refuse to attend the college, and also refuse to leave the country after their visa expires."

Eva looked at them in disgust.

Well, they could talk because they did not know what life was like back home, especially in an African country. Life is hard, no regular light, water, and food are expensive, going to school is hard, and if you try to even go to school, getting a job after is even harder. Most people thrive because they know people in higher positions. If one got an opportunity to leave the country, you definitely would not want to return. People will rather do a dirty job to feed themselves in the UK than remain back home.

Michael continued, "Now the College has put a lot of students who genuinely came to study in trouble."

All of this information was becoming too much for Eva to take in. She needed to get away from this discussion. Just as she plotted a reason to excuse herself, her phone rang. *Phew! Saved by the bell.* It was her auntie calling. It was past 8 pm already.

"Sophie, I need to be home now. It's past 8 pm."

"8 pm? Where did all the time go?"

Sophie too didn't realise it was that late already. They got up to leave. Sophie gave Eva a ride home while Richard dropped Michael off.

Throughout the ride home, Eva was worried but hid it from Sophie, so she started some small talk to help take her mind off her worry. For the first time, she was thankful she was disciplined enough not to discuss her status in the UK with Sophie. Now she had to look for other ways to tackle the situation, and this included looking up to God. She realized she had not talked to God about it since she heard the news.

Her default response in times like this was to go to God. She felt bad that she had made God her last port of call in this trying time when her mind was running into chaos.

Sophie was now at her front door. Eva was so glad to finally be alone with her thoughts.

Chapter Eight

Eva could barely sleep. Her mind was racing with thoughts of what the future held for her. If the College was found guilty, then her hopes and next step will be uncertain. Although not confirmed, what her auntie and Sophie's boyfriend said made her a little afraid. Eva eventually fell asleep. She dreamt she was on her night shift and just as she was handing over, a knock was heard at the door. It was the police and the immigration. They said they got a lead that some people were working illegally there. Eva was terrified and was about to get up when one of the officers stopped her to ask for her name and identity.

She trembled because she knew her visa was expired. Just as the officer proceeded to check her details, she woke up panting and sweating. *Thank goodness it was a dream!* She quickly went on her knees, praying and hoping that would never be her predicament.

Sleep eluded her. Eva was full of thoughts. She was thankful it was the weekend, so she had ample time to think and speak of her options with Auntie Tonia. She said her prayers and once it was bright enough, she went to discuss with her auntie, who was in the kitchen.

Eva narrated all that transpired the previous day, from the successful examinations to the unpleasant news she had heard later in the day. Her auntie was in shock as she listened. At first, she was speechless, then she composed herself and tried to allay Eva's worry about the possible outcome. However, she couldn't help but fear how this could affect Eva's stay in the UK.

"Let's wait and see what happens. You don't have to worry yourself sick. Everything will be sorted."

This made Eva feel at peace. Other members of the family were now awake and the house soon got busy. Eva decided to focus on what she had planned to do this weekend; part of which was to clean her room and go for her night shift job. As she made a mental note of her day's task, she remembered her early morning dream, and an overwhelming fear came over her. She shed it off quickly by praying.

Eva forgot all about the issue as she went on with her day. She loved working with the elderly at the Residential home. She enjoyed watching them tell their stories and experiences with no prejudice, especially Mrs. Batley, an African who got married to a white British man. She met him back in her country as a missionary who educated them. She smiled when she spoke of how theirs was a 'love at first sight' experience. She moved to the UK with him but struggled to fit in. It was hard to sort her settlement papers and even harder for the white folks to accept her. Racism was on a higher level back then than it is now. Despite all, the love for each other stayed strong and inseparable till he died a few years ago in his 90s.

The weekend was kind to Eva too. Church service this weekend was indeed a blessing. Eva could reconnect to God the way she did back in Nigeria. She decided to always stay connected and serve God, just as God expected from her. Sunday evening ended with the entire family visiting a family friend who lived in a city called Milton Keynes. Milton Keynes was on the outskirts of London with beautiful and quiet scenery. They were a lovely couple, with one child, who have stayed there for four years. The wife studied in the UK and met her husband at the University.

Eva found the place too fascinating. She needed to find out a thing or two more about the city.

"How expensive is it to live in Milton Keynes?"

"It's not so expensive to us because we have a good job," the lady responded evasively.

Eva admired the city, but she could only fantasize about what life was like there. They spent a few more hours and left.

Chapter Nine

It was Monday morning. Eva woke up with the worry of what will be the fate of her school. She prayed for God's peace and prepared to set out for school. Sophie had called to ask if she wanted a lift, but she told her not to pick her up today. She needed the alone time to think and prepare her mind for the next likely series of events. She arrived at school to meet a lot of students at the gate. She sighted Sophie in her car and went to sit with her. She asked to know what was going on, and the news she dreaded hit her. The school had been found guilty after the investigation.

It had been confirmed that they were running illegal activities, so the school had to be shut with immediate effect. The students would be transferred to another college, but it was not good news for those who needed to renew their visas. The school could no longer be of help as promised and have been black-listed at the home office.Eva felt the world collapse on her. She tried to keep her cool and not let her fear show on her face. After a while, she walked with Sophie towards a group of students being addressed by an official. He said practically the same thing Sophie had earlier told her. He added that a personal email would be sent to each student informing them of the next steps, including the different colleges they would be transferred to. It all sounded like a dream to Eva. She couldn't bring herself to make out the official's words. Her head was spinning. Her ears heard nothing. The students dispersed when the official finished talking. Some decided to go for a drink, while some went home. Sophie suggested that Eva and a few friends go for breakfast since it was still early. Eva preferred to go home or to just be alone. On second thought, she decided to be with them as this will help take her mind off these thoughts that were threatening to overwhelm her. They had breakfast at a nice restaurant on the College premises. They had been to this restaurant before, which was known for its tasty meals; but today the food seemed like sand forced into Eva's mouth. Swallowing was even more difficult, but in all, she tried to maintain composure.

They chatted about life and the possibilities ahead. They promised to keep in touch no matter what College they got transferred to and exchanged phone numbers and emails. Soon it was time to leave and Sophie offered to drop Eva, but she kindly declined. She wanted to visit one of her friends from work since there were no classes today. As Sophie dropped Eva at the bus stop, she took the bus to her friend's house.

Bisi was a friend she had met at the Residential home where she worked. She often spoke of how she survived for years without her legal papers here in the UK. Though Eva never disclosed her status, she always enjoyed Bisi's chatty company.

She was very kind too. Given Eva's current situation, she thought if it would help to share her situation with Bisi or just chat together over movies. She opted it was better to tell her and seek her opinion on what to do once her visa expires.

Bisi was chatty, as usual. She filled her in on what happened during her night shift at work and then talked about her boyfriend. Once she got up to get their food, Eva seized the opportunity to start the conversation.

"What do I do when my visa expires and I can't renew it?"

She let the words fall off her mouth.

Bisi stopped abruptly and turned back in shock.

"Eva, you never told me you're on visiting visa."

"No," Eva replied. "I have a Study Visa that I was planning to renew next month until we got the bad news from my College that they have been charged for fraud and illegally bringing people into the country. The government has ordered the immediate closure of the College so everyone who came in through the visa issued by the school obviously cannot renew their visa."

"Haa. That is not good news o. So would you go back to Nigeria or do you want to stay here?"

Eva thought deeply.

"Going home is not an option. Staying here too will be daunting as my visa expires soon."

"Hmm. There are many options, but first, I will tell you to keep your mouth shut about your status from now on. I think you have already been doing well in that regard because all the while I narrated my ordeal here in the UK to you, you never mentioned the type of visa you were on. I always thought you had a permanent stay, but anyway, we all are different. During my own time, I could not keep quiet and that landed me in trouble. A friend or someone I assumed to be my friend reported me to the authorities. I was arrested and detained but it took the grace of God to have me released back into society. What she meant for evil, God turned it around for good and used it to settle my stay here. Unfortunately, some people are not this lucky as they get deported to their various countries immediately."

"The next thing I will advise you is for you to get closer to God, as you will need Him more than before. My walk with Him grew when I had the problem. There were days I cried until I could cry no more. Some other days, all I did was listen to worship songs and pray in tongues because I was confused to the point that I couldn't pray in my understanding. Each time I tried to pray, bitterness took over, and instead of talking to God, I felt the urge to pray against the person who reported me to the authorities. But praying in tongues helped me a great deal. My advice to you would be to get closer and closer to God if you've not done that yet."

"Now, let's talk about the options. I will tell you all I was told, which I didn't fully accept as some of them were against my Christian beliefs. While some got away with it though probably living with the guilt, some were not lucky as they were caught before the last stage. I don't judge anyone, but I did what I knew God wanted me to do."

"I will tell you all the options I was given and leave you to make your choice. The first option was to have an arranged marriage. By this, you pay a European who pretends to marry you. The second option is to go back voluntarily with a travel document in another name. Then, get another visa with which you can come back.

The third option is to stay illegally and work with someone else's papers. The fourth option is to settle for manual jobs till after you have been here for 10yrs, then you can then properly apply for a visa. The last option would be to have a British boyfriend and get married legally."

Eva's head at this point was saturated. She was struggling to digest the overload of information all at once.

"I will suggest you speak to a good lawyer who will advise you properly. In the meantime, let's relax, eat and watch a movie. I promise you all will be well." Bisi's words sounded faintly in her head.

This was a lot for her to take in. She slouched into her seat.

Chapter Ten

Eva found Bisi's testimony encouraging. Though it wasn't her desire to be detained before getting her papers, she knew that if God could do it for Bisi, He would do it for her too. She felt better than she did earlier today at the College. She was now optimistic and had her mind at ease. They both watched the movie Bisi chose for them. Bisi had done this to take Eva's mind off the fear she came in with, and it worked as they now laughed as they discussed the movie.

Eva left Bisi's house with a lawyer's number she could call for help with her papers. She was eager to give her auntie updates on the situation, including this lawyer's number she had access to. Or perhaps she might have other options too.

When she got home, her auntie was not back yet, so she went to freshen up in her room and select her clothes for work the next day. As she was about to lie down, she heard her auntie's voice. She jumped off her bed and headed straight to the sitting room.

"Eva! Is there a problem? You're home early today."

Eva waited for her auntie to sit on her favorite couch and narrated everything that happened from the update with the College to the detailed conversation she had with Bisi later in the day. Her auntie had to interrupt her at different points in the narration as she was rambling on so quickly. She was tense yet positive. Her auntie agreed to speak with a lawyer friend she knew and together they would look into the options. That brought some relief to Eva. The thought that she had access to two lawyers who could help bring light at the end of this tunnel she found herself in was a great relief.

The next morning, Eva decided to go for a walk since there was no college to go to. She needed a few hours to think and get some fresh air. Ten minutes into her walk, she heard her phone ring. At first, she didn't want to pick, but she saw it was Michael and reluctantly picked it. She had not seen or spoken to him in a couple of days.

"Hello, Michael. How are you faring?"

"I'm doing well, thank you, Eva. I'm working on my transfer to one college in Milton Keynes. The College closure was a blessing in disguise for me. I never really liked London, so this presented an opportunity to move away from London. Milton Keynes seems like a better option for me, and I have some friends there too." He was excited to share the news with Eva.

"How about you? Have you got a College to move to?"

The last thing Eva wanted to do was to discuss her predicament with him, but she knew she had to say something.

"I don't know yet, but I'm sure my auntie will want me to stay in London. I'm not very certain of my next plans right now."

"Can we go out for a meal soon, if you don't mind?"

Eva was not in the mood for a date, a meal, or a boyfriend. However, she knew she needed some break from her thoughts.

"Not a bad idea. Is Saturday okay with you?"

"Yeah. That's okay with me. I will pick you at 4 pm."

They had some more small talk and said their goodbyes. Eva felt relaxed as she talked with Michael. She feels she likes him but doesn't know much about him other than the few stories he had told her before.

As Eva walked, her thoughts were all about what the future possibly held for her and Michael, if there was any at all. One thing she was sure of was that they would remain very good friends for a long time. Whilst in College, he came to see her regularly.

He sometimes brought her lunch or took her to the College cafe and paid for the meal. Paying for a friend's meal was something hardly done here. The first time he brought her lunch, she offered to pay back his money, but he refused.

"Ah, I am African, and we don't ask a lady to pay. Even if we are in the western world, I still respect my African training," he had said.

He was such a gentleman. Eva snapped out of her thoughts and played some music on the phone. She sang along while praying in her mind for God to show up for her in this and all situations.

As Eva stepped inside from her walk, she heard her aunt's voice talking to her children. She eagerly rushed to ask her if she got to speak with the lawyer as promised. Her auntie thought that was rude and interrupted her.

"Can't you say hello first before putting me under scrutiny?"

"I'm sorry, auntie. Good afternoon. How was your day?"

Her auntie smiled and said, "Thank you ma, my day was great."

Eva then calmed down and asked if she could help her with anything. She was itching to hear the outcome of the call with the lawyer, but her auntie was clearly not ready to talk yet. Eva tried to take her mind off the thoughts. She offered to assist Sister Bose in making dinner.

Sister Bose was happy to have Eva with her in the kitchen, not because she wanted her to help, but just so she would have company.

"Why didn't you go to the College today?"

Eva was thrown back into her thoughts. *Why did I even volunteer to help in the kitchen?*

She wasn't sure if it was safe to tell sister Bose the truth yet or she should still keep quiet. Her auntie had told her not to tell anybody or talk about her predicament.

"I have finished all my exams, and the College asked us to stay at home for now as they were sorting some things out."

At least I didn't have to lie.

"Oh. So will I see you more often now or would you take more shifts at work? My friend's daughter always took more shifts once she was on break in College. My friend would complain that the girl was not staying at home, that her daughter was more concerned with making money than spending time with family."

"I don't know yet." She let out a burst of loud laughter at the story Sister Bose just told her.

Deep in her mind, she considered this to be a good idea, though. She could make more money before deciding on the option to follow to renew her visa. She was so deep in thoughts that she didn't hear her auntie's voice call her.

"Auntie is calling you." Sister Bose had to tap her.

"Are you okay?"

Eva jumped and said, "I'm okay. Did you say auntie is calling me?"

"Yes. She's been calling you for a while."

"Oh. Ok. Thanks." Eva replied and went to see her auntie.

Chapter Eleven

"Why did it take you so long to answer me?"

"I'm sorry I was lost in thought."

Her auntie interjected, "You have been doing that lately. You better not kill yourself with worry. There is nothing God cannot solve. What is happening to you now has happened to few other persons, and they scaled through, so you are not the first and you won't be the last."

As she was speaking, Auntie Tonia's phone rang. She signalled for Eva to excuse her while she answered the call.

Eva was not happy. She was expecting her auntie to give her the lawyer's feedback. She had to wait yet again. Eva was practically counting the seconds of the clock as she waited for her auntie to get off the phone. The call was taking too long. *Or is she playing with my emotions?*

She left for her room and thought to pray instead. She had been too busy thinking, worrying, and trying to find solutions herself, rather than praying. She knelt and took her bible to read and pray. She had slept for 30mins when she heard a knock on her door.

"Come in."

It was Sister Bose.

"Are you ready to eat? Food is ready."

The rest of the family went on with dinner when she delayed in joining them. Her nephew was sent to call her but said he heard her praying and didn't want to disturb her.

"Thank you. I will come and eat. Is auntie still in the sitting room or she's gone to sleep?" she asked Sister Bose.

"She is watching a movie with her husband."

Eva got her food and sat to eat at the dining table. She peeked into the sitting room area and saw her auntie engrossed in the movie. The prayer did her good, as she didn't feel any worry in her mind anymore. She left the matter in God's good hands.

She read through the several messages she had ignored on her phone while enjoying her meal. Michael had called. He left her four missed calls and several messages. She smiled. *This guy's calls are becoming too much? Does he not have things to do? A tall, kind, and handsome guy like Michael cannot possibly be without a girlfriend? Who knows? He's probably one of those players. I'm not interested in joining the girlfriends' list, please. Being a friend is just fine for me.*

She responded to a few of his messages. He had to cancel their outing on Saturday because he had to go to Milton Keynes. The College he enrolled in had sent a mail invite for an interview on Friday. He also had to attend the Open day for the new students on Saturday, as all new students were expected to be present. He requested that their outing be rescheduled for either Sunday or Monday evening when he would be back. Eva wasn't having any of it, though. *What does this guy even think of me? He's probably going off with a girl for the weekend and then he comes up with these lines?*

"It's fine, Michael. We may have to think of another day. I have to be at work on those days." She texted her reply.

She had taken a cue from what Sister Bose said. She took more shifts, so she practically worked every day. She continued to reply to all other messages, including returning Bisi's call, who wanted to find out if she was coming to work the next day. They agreed to go to work together since they were on the same shift. Bisi would pick her up on the way. At least she now had something to look forward to. She enjoyed working with Bisi. It automatically meant enough gist through the night to keep them from sleeping.

Eva waited for a while, hoping her auntie would call her so they could have the talk. However, after an hour with no call, she forgot about it and went to her room. She knew her auntie would talk when she was ready, but in the meantime, she would be at peace and enjoy herself. She watched some movies to keep her mind occupied.

She woke up to a knock on her door the next morning. She wasn't expecting anyone that early, as she was not going out today. She did not have to help Bose with any chore either, so what was the knock for? In fact, she had stayed up late the previous night as she already planned to stay late in bed this morning.

She heard the knock again and asked, "Who is it? Come in."

It was her auntie.

Eva jumped up.

"Good morning, auntie. Is everything okay? Do you need me to do something?"

"No. I wanted to speak with you before I leave for work."

She came into Eva's room and sat on the chair beside the window.

"I'm sorry I didn't get to talk to you yesterday. It was because I don't have a concrete answer for you yet, neither do I have any good news, but I can see that you will not rest until you hear from me, so I thought to share what the lawyer told me."

She continued, "He said there are different options. One, you can go back and try to apply for your renewal from there, although that is not guaranteed. Two, you have an arranged wedding, which you know I will not approve of. Three, you try to apply here, but that would be hard as they would usually ask you to go back voluntarily first. The last option would be to lie low for the next ten to fourteen years."

Eva was now wide awake. She didn't like what she heard at all. She sincerely wanted to just break down and cry because none of the options was good enough for her, but she kept calm and trusted God to lead her to the right solution.

"I will speak to another person who went through a similar predicament. But in the meantime, I want you to be optimistic and trust God to show us what to do. I will be on my way now." Her auntie's voice interrupted her thoughts.

"Are you working tonight?"

"Yes, I am."

"Alright. Bye." And she left her with her thoughts.

Eva struggled with going back to sleep. Her aunt's voice kept echoing in her head. She decided to go for a walk to clear her mind. As she got dressed, she heard her phone ring. It was Sophie. It had been a couple of weeks since they last spoke.

"Hello Sophie," she was eager to hear the latest updates.

"Hi, Eva. How are you doing?"

"I'm doing well, Sophie. What's up?"

"I have enrolled in a new college in the city. How about you? How did your transfer go?"

Eva did not want to lie.

"I have not started looking for any yet. I need to first renew my visa before sorting my transfer."

"Are you considering staying in London? I remember you talked about moving to Milton Keynes or Scotland before the whole College saga."

Eva giggled.

"I have not given that thought since after the last time we spoke about it. You remember my friend, Michael. He's moving to Milton Keynes to continue his college. I'm sure if I also decide to go to Milton Keynes, he will be the happiest person ever." She laughed out loud.

Sophie joined in the laughter.

"Are you starting a relationship with him?"

"No. He asked me out on a date but cancelled because he had to go for the enrolment exercise at the new college in Milton Keynes."

"I think he's a good guy. You should give him a chance."

"That's not on my mind now. I just want to get my College transfer sorted and then work to make more money."

"How about your boyfriend?" Eva asked Sophie.

"He's fine."

They chatted some more and hung up.

Chapter Twelve

Eva left the house with her earpiece to listen to some music. She enjoyed listening to music or a sermon while on a walk. The music or sermon often helped her reflect on her life. Sister Bose had asked her on her way out if she would like some breakfast, to which she politely declined.

"I really need to get on this walk as fast as possible before I change my mind. I will get something to eat when I return."

"Okay, I will be out by the time you get back. There is jollof rice and chicken stew in the fridge if you want."

Eva thanked her and left.

Her mind was filled with several thoughts. *If not for the hardship back home in Nigeria, bad governance, limited work for graduates, poor living, no one will think of leaving the country.* The hardship was just too much for her parents and she was beginning to feel like a burden to them. Since she finished her OND, there was no money to continue her studies, and that had made her depressed. Some of her friends could further their careers, but for her, she had to stop. With four younger ones who needed to get basic education until SS3 at least, hers became of least priority.

When the opportunity came for her to travel, she had grabbed it quickly, hoping once she got here, she would be able to help her parents and siblings. She was so happy and grateful that God had answered her prayer, though what she was going through right now was not a part of the plan. One thing she remained very sure of was that though the journey seemed hard, it would end well. Her faith was secured in God.

It was sunny and hot. She made her choice of music and plugged her ears to cancel out the noise from her surroundings. All she could hear was her music and heartbeat. For the first hour, she hummed along to the music, completely oblivious to her surroundings until she heard a car hoot that she noticed she had walked into the road.

Eva jumped in fear.

"I'm sorry."

She used only one of her earpieces instead to avoid another scenario. She continued her walk while thinking of what her auntie told her. She weighed all the options and thought the option of lying low was the best and only option for her. She also worried about how she would survive that option.

From what Auntie Tonia had explained to her, that option meant losing her voice, as she would resort to limited interactions with people, and probably take up a new identity. It meant few or no friends at all because she had to be careful of people who might report her to the authorities. Also, she would probably have to move to another city and start a new life. Hopefully, she would find a man to marry before the ten to fourteen-year period elapsed, and then attempt to apply for her permanent stay.

Hmmm.

She said a quick prayer in her heart for God's guidance on this journey. *God, help me to endure and not commit a sin out of desperation. What city will I move to?*

Milton Keynes was her first option, but being close to Michael was not the best option, as this could cloud her decision. The other city she had visited was Scotland, so she was limited to these two cities, except her auntie knew anyone else in another city.

I'll have to discuss this with my aunt. Her thought immediately switched to Michael. An easy way out was to acknowledge Michael's interest in her and accept his proposal to date him. If she coaxed him into marrying her, her visa would be automatically sorted, since he was British. *But is this what God wants for me? Why should I get married just for papers? Why should I marry without love?* She battled these thoughts in her head and concluded that this wasn't how she pictured getting married.

Dating Michael for the sake of papers was out of the option.

In the meantime, she worked more shifts so she could save more money before her visa expired. She needed to be prepared for the uncertainty of the coming year.

Enough of the mental calculations, Eva, breathe.

She took in a deep breath and spent the rest of her walk just enjoying the music. She was now singing out so loud she didn't realize until someone came next to her and looked to see if she was okay.

"Can I help you?" she asked, unaware of her loud voice.

"Your voice is quite loud."

"Oh, I'm sorry."

She immediately thought of how different our cultures were. If you sang out loud that way back in Nigeria, people would just assume you were crazy or you were probably showing off, but you were sure that no one would confront you. She reduced the music volume and her voice so she doesn't create a nuisance. She had done two things today to clear her heavy and unsettled mind.

Eva decided it was now time to head back home. She was tired, hungry, and would need some rest before her evening shift at work. Her recent days have been from one worry to another. The reality of what people who travelled had to go through gradually dawned on her.

No one ever told her it was hard here in 'the abroad' as it was called. This life with no identity and voice was not what she bargained for. However, she secured her trust in God to see her through in this new phase of life ahead of her.

Chapter Thirteen

Few weeks down the line, there was still no solution in sight. The option of starting a new life in another city still seemed like the route she had to take. Losing her voice and identity until her visa was sorted were the perks of this new life, but she had no choice.

After much deliberation, her auntie decided Manchester was the best city for her to go to. She knows a family there who needed a childminder.

They would provide her with a place to stay while paying her a salary. It sounded like a good opportunity, though she never thought she would have to take on a child-minding role. She, however, knew that whatever experience God allowed her to go through, it was necessary so she could help others who also have to face it.

This journey was hers and she would walk through it with God on her side. All will be well.

She was scheduled to leave in two weeks, so she used the remaining weeks and days to get together with her friends and work a bit more.

Her phone rang. It was Michael. It had been a while since she last spoke to him because she had been avoiding him. At this point though, she felt she needed to keep him in the loop of her plans.

"Hi Michael," she said. "How are you?"

Michael sounded so excited to hear her voice.

"Hey Eva, how are you? You have not been picking my calls. Did I do something wrong? If I did, I am sorry, please."

"No, no, you did nothing wrong. It's just been a difficult and tiring time." She interrupted him to explain.

She wasn't sure how far she should go in telling him the full details. A part of her felt her secrets were safe with him. She trusted him, so she told him all about it.

Some minutes into the conversation, Michael cut her short.

"Eva, I don't think this should be a telephone conversation. Can we meet over a meal this weekend?"

Eva knew in her heart that she truly needed that outing.

"Yes, that's fine. I don't work on Saturdays."

"I will pick you up. I've started driving, so it would be easy for me to travel in and out of London now.

"Okay, I'll be looking forward to it."

They talked some more before hanging up. Michael told her about his new life at Buckingham University. He had secured his admission through the Foundation route instead of going through College. It was an excellent step for him and he was overjoyed about it. He also talked about his place of residence. He lived with four other guys, two whites and two black guys. They got along really well. It was a big house with a gym area in it for the residents.

Eva did not hide her genuine happiness for him. Michael was stepping into the life he desired already and in quick succession. He is very hardworking and ambitious, knows what he wants, and goes for it. She was lost in thoughts about him again. *Come off it, Eva.* She smiled as she jolted herself back to reality. Truth is, she had grown to really like him and that was the reason she didn't want to be in close contact with him these few days she had before leaving London. She didn't want to miss him while away in Manchester. But when she saw his call today, she could not ignore his call, and she was glad she didn't.

By the time they said their goodbyes, they had spent almost 5hours. Their conversation was a breath of fresh air for her. Saturday was definitely a date. Nothing would stop it.

Chapter Fourteen

"Good morning, Eva. Auntie wants to speak with you."

Sister Bose said to Eva through her closed door.

Eva was clueless about what the call was for. The last few days have been spent getting her ready for her trip. There was so much activity she had to keep up with. She encouraged herself not to entertain any worry or fear. She would embark on this journey with trust in God.

When she got to her auntie, she handed her an envelope.

"It's a small token from me and my husband. We trust you will spend your money wisely. Have this for your upkeep so you wouldn't have to disturb the family you'll be staying with, pending when you get your first salary."

She didn't know how to stop the tears that flowed from her eyes. Her auntie and uncle have been good to her. They had already taken her to shop for clothes over the weekend, now they were giving her money. She will forever appreciate her auntie's family. Her auntie's family didn't leave her to cater to herself because she had a job already.

The savings she had made helped her send money monthly to her family back in Nigeria. Things had not turned out the way she expected, but God has been good to her. She wiped her eyes continually to stop the flow of tears.

"Thank you so much, auntie. You and Uncle have done so much for me, and I'm more than grateful, auntie." She said in a teary voice.

"It's okay. We are always happy to help you."

"We will drive you to Manchester and stay in a hotel together for the weekend so you can settle before moving to your new family. They are a good family so you don't have to be worried about anything."

Eva thanked her and left for her room to put her items together.

As she got in her room, still with teary eyes, she remembered how they lost contact with this auntie of hers for years. Her mum tried every means to locate her, especially when things were hard, but to no avail. After nearly giving up, her mum received a call from her one day, explaining that she had lost her mum's phone number.

She said she had retrieved her number from one of her mum's old friends she met in the UK. She was so happy to reconnect with her that right there she promised to come and visit them before the year ran out and, true to her words, she came down to Nigeria for Christmas. Since then, she had been of immense support to her family.

The next year, she came back to take Eva to the UK. Eva sat and marvelled at how God could orchestrate one's journey in life. Here she was, about to leave her auntie's family for another she didn't know but had been assured of their kindness. She opened the envelope and, to her surprise, she found £1000 inside. She was shocked. How can they be this generous to her?

One time she thanked her auntie for all the love she showed her, her auntie said it does not compare to what Eva's mum did for her. She said her mum was the reason she was in the UK today. Eva's mum sold all she had to send her to school till university and finally sent her abroad, so whatever she did now could still not quantify what her mummy did for her.

Eve was still shocked, especially as they knew how much she had in her bank account, yet they were being this generous to her. She closed the envelope and said a prayer for their finances and their business. She also prayed for the family she was going to.

The next day, Eva decided she would open up to her auntie about Michael. Her auntie always made her feel free to talk about anything with her. She was considering accepting Michael's request to take their friendship to the next level, so she felt this was the best time to tell her auntie.

Her auntie had just returned from work, so she waited for her to settle before asking if she could have a word with her.

"Let's go to the garden," she told Eva.

Eva told her auntie everything about Michael from when she met him to date. She also talked about how she felt about Michael and her intention to accept his request.

Her auntie smiled.

"I have been waiting for the day you would tell me about this friend of yours. I have noticed the way you always light up when you talk to him or when you tell Sophie about him. I didn't want to be too forward but wait till when you were ready to talk about it. I'm happy that you're honest with me about it. You have my full support."

"Is it okay for me to tell Michael the truth about my situation when we meet up on Saturday?" Eva asked.

"That's ok. It's always good to be honest in a relationship from the start."

Eva was so excited. She tried to hide her emotions, but her auntie could tell.

"Auntie Eva, we were looking for you. Are you going to read to us tonight?" Tobi and Dumininu came running towards Eva and her aunt.

"Of course, I won't miss that for anything," Eva responded.

Auntie tried to hold back the tears that were fast filling her eyes. She felt for the children. They would miss their auntie Eva they had now grown so fond of. Auntie Tonia had not been able to tell them Eva was leaving. She didn't want to upset them.

Eva left with the children, leaving her auntie in the garden with her thoughts. They met their uncle at the door as they stepped inside the house.

"Where is auntie?"

Eva pointed to the garden. "Over there."

He went to meet her.

Eva was happy. *Auntie would need some company right now.*

Chapter Fifteen

The next day, Eva went to work. It would be her last day working there. She had told a few of her colleagues that she was moving to Manchester. Some were nosey and wanted to know why she was moving that far, but Bisi had rehearsed with her the perfect response to give to anyone who asked. She would tell them she was going to stay with another family of hers where she would continue her studies.

Bisi told her she would pick her up 2hours before resumption time. When Eva asked why, she said she needed to do some stuff before their shift starts. As she got ready, she thought of how much she would miss Bisi.

They have grown so close since she shared her situation with her. Bisi has been so supportive, ensuring she didn't get into depression from worrying. She took her out for meals. She also bought a set of earrings and a necklace which was very expensive but she wanted Eva to always look at them whenever she missed her or felt lonely. She promised to pay her a visit in Manchester.

She heard a knock on her door. It was Auntie Tonia.

"Are you ready?" she asked.

She spotted the outfit Eva had on the bed to wear.

"Why don't you wear something different and nicer since it's your last day? You might want to take pictures with your colleagues who are around. It's a late shift so there's likely to be more staff around."

"Ok, that's a good idea, auntie."

She quickly changed before Bisi came. She wore a nice pair of black trousers with one of the beautiful tops her auntie recently bought for her.

As she was putting on her shoes, she heard Bisi's car horn. She quickly grabbed her bag, saying goodbye to everyone.

Bisi's eyes lit up as she saw her.

"Wow, you are looking beautiful. I like what you are wearing."

She teased her, "If only Michael can see you today, maybe he will propose immediately." They both laughed.

When they arrived at the office, Bisi asked her to please go inside and call Clara to come to pick up some stuff from her car. It seemed weird to Eva. *Couldn't that wait till later? Was Bisi going somewhere after dropping her? Why did they even have to be at the office 2 hours earlier?* Well, she pushed her thoughts aside and went in to call Clara.

Just as she opened the door, the sound of 'SURPRISE!!!!!!' hit her. She jumped back in shock, not sure who the surprise was for until she saw Bisi behind her smiling. She also saw a banner with her name on it. So this was why Bisi was acting weird and why her auntie insisted she dressed nicely today.

That means her auntie knew about it too. She didn't know when the tears started rolling down as each person hugged her. She would miss the friends she had made here. She never thought she would leave them this soon and she could not still tell them the true situation of things.

Bisi handed her a tissue and moved her toward a table that had different cards and gifts. She was so overwhelmed with so much love from staff and even the residents. She got a huge gift from her best resident, who loves her so much. She was crying when Eva went to hug her, telling her how much she will miss her. Eva promised to always call to talk with her, which brought a smile to her pretty old face.

There were lots to eat. The staff had all volunteered to bring food. Bisi and a Nigerian staff made some Nigerian delicacies too. After some time, she was given a chance to talk, and she thanked everybody for their love and the surprise party. Though the usual life of the party, she was short of words this time. She never had people do this kind of thing for her.

There were different kind remarks of how kind she was. She thanked God for moulding her into such a person who did what she had to do without waiting for a reward.

They had a good time, took pictures, and sang till her shift started.

Chapter Sixteen

When she got home, her family was amazed at the number of gifts and cards Eva received. Her uncle didn't seem surprised, anyway. He thought Eva was a genuinely kind person who deserved all she got. Bisi and the children helped to move the items to her room.

Later that night, Sister Bose came to her room to have a chat. Since she got to know of the situation, she always encouraged her to look away from the negative part of the situation, but trust God to bring out the best in it.

Eva expected Sister Bose had come in to speak with her like she usually did. But today was different. Sister Bose came in with a small bag she gave to Eva, smiling.

"This is my little gift and I hope you like it."

Eva opened it and was so happy to see the content. It was a lovely traditional dress, just like the ones worn in Nigeria.

Sister Bose looked at her as she jumped, expressing her thanks. She absolutely loved traditional wears.

"I sewed it personally for you. I had to keep hiding it so you wouldn't see it before it was ready."

Eva hugged her tightly.

"I will wear it to church on Sunday."

It would be her last Sunday in the church. Some people knew she was leaving, though they didn't know why. She also spared them the details except for the ones who were bold enough to ask; and all she told them was that she was moving to stay with another family while continuing her studies.

Sister Bose was happy she could gift her the dress. Eva was so happy and tired from the activities of the day. The children wanted to help unwrap her gifts, but she told them they would do it tomorrow as she wanted to go to bed early.

She was changing into her nightwear when her phone rang. Without looking at the phone, she was sure it was Michael. It has been his ritual these days to call her late in the night before she sleeps. He always called to ask how her day went and sometimes they prayed together. It's funny the rush of energy she felt whenever Michael called.

She always looked forward to his call and hoped her move to Manchester would not stop their midnight call. It may likely reduce, but she didn't want it to stop completely.

Michael wanted to be the one to take her to Manchester but her auntie had already made plans to do that and stay the weekend with her, so that was not possible. Michael was a little hurt he couldn't spend the last hours with her. Well, he would see her on Saturday, anyway.

He promised to make it a very significant date for him. They talked on for like two hours, prayed together, and said goodnight.

That night, she was filled with mixed feelings. The thoughts of leaving her family here while thinking about what it will be like living in the new place. It was a struggle to sleep, so she played some music to distract her from her thoughts

After a few hours, she drifted off to sleep.

Chapter Seventeen

Her outing with Michael went very well. She felt so comfortable in his presence. They had a pleasant time together. She knew Michael was going to pop the question regarding their relationship, but a part of her thought he would develop cold feet, especially with the news of her moving far away. Michael wanted to know every detail about her. Eva told him the exact situation of things without holding back. Michael was speechless and looked unhappy.

After a few minutes, he asked, "Is there any other way around this so you don't have to move?"

Eva gave a breakdown of all the options she had been given as alternative ways to get her visa renewed.

Michael jumped at the marriage option.

"Then let's get married right away!"

Eva smiled.

"I can't do that. I will not marry just because I want to renew my visa. That is against my belief. I will marry for the right reason. I refuse to get married in a rush."

Michael truly liked to have her as a life partner, but he knew he couldn't change Eva's stance on the matter.

"I believe everything will end well." Eva tried to sound optimistic.

"Can I ask you a question?" Michael braced himself up.

Eva knew what the question was, but she allowed him to finish.

"What is your response to my former question?"

Eva smiled, "I have thought about it and I am ready to give it a go if you still want to."

"Of course, I want nothing more than that. From the very first day I saw you, I knew you will be a special person in my life." Michael said to her with a shimmer of excitement in his eyes.

"Now you are moving to Manchester, how will I be able to see you?"

"I will definitely like you to come over to visit once I settle down and get to know the family well."

"I have also told my auntie about you," Eva added.

She could see Michael's face light up as he heard that. He felt special and truly accepted by Eva.

"Thank you," he said to her, blushing.

"What for?"

"For mentioning me to your auntie. I am sure you must have thought it through before doing that."

The rest of the evening was fun. They talked about what the future possibly held for them. The journey back home was with mixed feelings. Michael was glad he now knew where he stood with Eva. He also felt pain in his heart as this would be the last he would see her till he can visit her in Manchester. He savoured every minute of it. Michael dropped her home and bade her goodbye.

Once Eva opened the door, her auntie jumped.

"Hmmm. Is that our Michael?"

Eva was embarrassed as she didn't know her auntie was looking through the window.

She smiled, "yes".

As she turned to leave for her room, her phone rang. It was Bisi. Eva knew she was calling to hear about the outing.

"Are you home? Oya, gist me."

Eva laughed, "You couldn't even wait for tomorrow?"

"No o. The earlier, the better. Let's strike the iron while it's hot."

Eva told her how the night went. They were not going on with marriage plans yet till she gets to Manchester.

"DO you see yourself marrying this guy in the future?

"It hasn't gotten to that now," Eva replied playfully.

"Let me advise you. If you love or at least like him, try to keep him. The way you talk about him, I think he is a good guy and means well for you. Guys like that are hard to find. Don't let distance create a problem between you two. Who knows? We might just be planning your wedding in a few years from now."

"Thank you, my chief planner," Eva laughed.

"When you get to Manchester, please choose your friends wisely. Don't talk too much or tell people about your situation. You are in a new city and you are starting a new identity because your old identity must be kept quiet till you can sort your papers." Bisi chipped in some advice.

"Please keep in touch. Try to write all your contacts out in a book or diary in case they decide to change your number. Make sure you call me immediately you get there. I will miss you but I wish you the best and will continue to pray for you." She ended the call.

The next day in church was quite emotional as the few friends she made rallied around to pray for her and give her few gifts. They all appreciated her contributions and would miss her kind nature. They took several pictures. She looked so lovely in the dress Sister Bose made her.

Chapter Eighteen

The remaining days were spent in quietness and a reflective mood. She was looking forward to the journey, except for the fact that she might lose her identity. Auntie Tonia had told her she might not use her real name once she got there. This did not sit well with her. She had to do what she had to do, anyway. She just hoped that things would get sorted soon and her life would return to normal.

Her auntie said they would leave on Friday morning. She informed the children's school that they would be absent on Friday.

Eva woke up earlier than her usual time. She was tense. Thankfully, the entire family would be going with her rather than riding alone on the train. It was a fun ride to Manchester. It was a mini adventure for her as she got to know many new cities.

They stopped twice at Service to get something to eat, and to stretch their legs. They also needed to use the toilet. The journey was so long that Eva thought it would be tough to run back to London even if she ever wanted to.

When they got to Manchester, they first dropped Eva's stuff at the new family's house and did some small acquaintance, after which they all went back to the hotel with Eva.

They wanted to spend the night with her, take her around Manchester the next day, being Saturday before taking her finally to the family.

The new family was so happy to meet Eva and her family. They gave them a warm reception. They had twin babies, the children Eva would be caring for.

They showed her to her room, which was big and had a desk and table.

Eva wondered why there was a desk and table in it, but she was happy as she could study the books she brought. After exchanging pleasantries and a brief tour around the house, the lady of the house named Ruth set the table for them all to eat.

The husband also had a welcoming personality. They are Christians and regular churchgoers. Eva was introduced as Kemi which was her middle name. She would be referred to as Kemi from now on. She was a bit happy that it was still her name and her mother's favourite name she called her, so she still felt some connection with the name.

The food was nice. She enjoyed the few hours she spent with them. Lady Ruth didn't seem like a talker, but her husband was the life of the party.

After the meal, he and Eva's uncle went to chat in the sitting room while the ladies all went into the kitchen. The kitchen was huge. In fact, the entire house was big and beautiful.

Auntie Ruth took Eva and her auntie around the house. They saw the babies' room, which was next to Eva's room. Auntie Ruth said the babies' monitor will be in Eva's room so she won't have to sleep in their room.

Auntie Ruth works as a social worker while Uncle Niyi was a medical doctor; a consultant in the big hospital in the city. They were happy Eva could come because Auntie Ruth was scheduled to resume work in a few weeks. Eva's coming will help her learn how to care for the babies with Auntie Ruth's guide.

After spending a few hours, Eva's auntie requested that they take their leave for the hotel. Auntie Ruth tries to persuade them to let Eva stay, but she kindly declines because they have promised the children that Eva will be with them for the night and they would be going out together tomorrow.

When they got to the hotel, they talked about the family. They all affirmed their kindness and prayed they stayed like that. Eva's auntie gave her a new sim card with a new number and she helped her transfer her contacts to it. Eva chatted with Michael on the new number that night. She also sent it to Bisi.

The next day, they went on a tour of the city and had lunch in one of the restaurants at the city centre. It was a cool place with a lovely ambience. Eva liked what she saw and hoped that even in her new identity, she will learn to love this city.

Later in the evening, they took Eva to her new home, and they went back to the hotel. They got the address of Auntie Ruth's church and promised to fellowship with them the next day, Sunday.

Eva's first night was a bit weird. She found it difficult to sleep and didn't want to call Michael so she does not disturb the house talking in the night.

She used the few hours to unpack her stuff and spent the rest of the time with the babies who warmed up to her like they had known her forever. She also loves children. This gave Auntie Ruth Joy.

The next day they went early to church as they said they had to attend Workers' Meeting before the main service started. Eva, now called Kemi, was shown a room where she could stay with the babies. She liked the church. It was bigger than their London church.

Once the workers' meeting finished, Auntie Ruth introduced Kemi to everyone as her little sister, though not biologically. Most Nigerians called people younger than them by 'sister' or 'brother'. Everyone was friendly to her and introduced themselves.

Eva's family arrived just in time for the main service. Tobi and Dumininu ran to Eva and hugged her so much. Her auntie told Eva that the children cried so much last night when Eva left. Eva had to assure them she would call them regularly and make out time to come see them. This brightened their mood. The church service was great. They all enjoyed it.

After service, Eva's family bade her goodbye and promised to come and see her soon. Seeing them leave brought tears to her eyes, but she tried to hide it so the children won't cry. They hugged her so much that they didn't want to leave. Their mum had to promise them some chocolate and ice cream on the way before they let go.

Chapter Nineteen

Life as Kemi started on a pleasant note. Auntie Ruth and Uncle Niyi were so nice to her. Kemi settled well in the new city. The church became a family for her, where she was accepted and loved.

The first week she was home, mostly doing the cleaning of the house and food preparation. Auntie Ruth liked to cook so Kemi only helped once in a while. Caring for the twins was not too hard for her. The children were lovely and peaceful.

Getting inducted into her tasks was pretty smooth. Auntie Ruth was still on maternity leave, so Kemi had sufficient time to understand the daily routine with the babies, house chores, and meal prep.

They also went to the market together, but Auntie Ruth told her not to take the bus for now as that would be tough while pushing the twins in the pushchair. For now, they would do the food shopping together. She, however, showed her how to catch the bus or tram to town so that on her day off she could go round the town.

She soon made a new friend called Anne who had lived all her life in Manchester but spoke fluent Yoruba. They met in the children's church where Kemi stayed with the twins and bonded as friends from the first day. Anne was a children's church teacher, so they met when she came into the children's church with the twins.

Anne introduced herself, asking her a few questions because it was her first time seeing Kemi. They bonded well because Anne ` was quite a talker like Kemi, so they had something in common. Kemi was still very cautious not to divulge too much information. Anne volunteered to take Kemi around Manchester any day she wanted. They exchanged numbers, and she promised to call her later. Coincidentally, she lived close to Auntie Ruth and had helped babysit a few times, and during church service.

Auntie Tonia had given her a bank account she was not using so she could make it her salary account since she couldn't use her other account. She also helped her transfer all her money to the new account, leaving just a small amount in the old one to keep it open. She gave her old bank card to her auntie Tonia so nothing would trace her to her new city.

The city seemed like London, busy as well with many people. You could get lost in it if not careful. Michael called her regularly, but not every night like they used to. However, their friendship grew stronger beyond their imagination.

This was a surprise to both of them as they genuinely thought the distance would cause a strain, but so far, it had not. They prayed together regularly too. Michael still held on to his promise to visit her once she settled.

After a few months, Auntie Ruth and Uncle Niyi enrolled her in an online course. She could continue her studies, much to her delight. She was treated like their biological sister. They ensured she lacked nothing.

Chapter Twenty

She continued her discreet life in Manchester while managing to make few friends. Whenever she went out with her new family and sighted a policeman, intense fear gripped her. In those moments, she encouraged herself in God's word to keep her safe.

Any knock on the door made her heart skip with fear. She immediately thought someone had reported her and the immigration officers had come to arrest her. She had some good days, but some other days were filled with overwhelming emotions.

As was her practice back in London, she often used music to suppress her thoughts. The children kept her busy too. They were playful in a way that eased her tensed emotions.

Life as an illegal immigrant is not the best and should not be experienced by anybody. Eva could not do a lot of things. She could not have access to a GP. She often prayed not to have to go to the hospital.

Thankfully, her schedule didn't require a regular commute, else that would have been a challenge.

To buy a weekly or monthly bus, she needed to have a Photo ID which was not accessible to illegal immigrants.

She got only one day off work every week, so she didn't require a weekly pass. She sometimes went with Anne and a few friends to town, and that was possible with a day bus pass. On some other days, she walked to Anne's house if Anne was not working.

Through Anne and the church, she made new friends, including a lovely Asian girl who also lived close to her house. Apart from the limitation she had to face because of an absence of papers to work, she was grateful for the happy family she had around her.

She often heard some other people's stories, how they could not work and had no money coming in for them and had to depend on people for money.

Some even ended up sleeping on the street because they could not afford money to pay for accommodation. These experiences made her see reasons to thank God for always being there for her.

She joined the choir in church. When she had to minister, Anne helped her look after the twins. Sometimes, Auntie Ruth took her to choir practice with the twins. Everyone was always warm to her and the babies, lending their support whenever she needed them. Life without a voice was hard, but God had made a way for her through it all, so she had reasons to praise His name.

Chapter Twenty-one

Time had rolled really fast. It was now a year since she moved to Manchester. Auntie Ruth and the family needed to travel, so they asked Kemi if she wanted to stay alone at home or if she didn't mind having Anne come to stay over with her or she would go to Anne's house. She and Anne had become so close, but she still held back from disclosing her status to her. Anne sometimes asked her questions, but she always knew how to evade them. No other person in Manchester could match her relationship with Sophie, Bisi, and Michael. With them, she was always free and happy. She lived a rather quiet life here.

Michael had not been able to visit her since she arrived, but they always did video calls to make them feel close. Michael had promised to visit this year's summer, and she's really looked forward to summer. Her auntie and uncle also called her regularly, and she got to speak with the children.

They suggested she should either come visiting on her next off day or they would come. They wanted her to settle well in her new place before suggesting that she come visiting.

Bisi keeps her up to date with happenings in London and at work. She had plans to go to Nigeria for a holiday after a long time. She had got into a romantic relationship which she sensed was leading to marriage. Kemi was so happy for her. She was pleased to hear good news from her old friends.

Kemi preferred to stay alone at home when Auntie Ruth and Uncle Niyi travelled. She had now mastered her way around the city. She had been going to town by herself and even went to the church's midweek service on the bus. Her friendship with Anne and the others had helped her settle well.

After much thought, she asked Auntie Ruth and her husband if it was okay for her to go to London whilst they were away. They agreed to her request. She was so happy and quickly informed Michael that she would come to London. It was a perfect arrangement, as the children would be on holiday. That meant sufficient time to spend with them. She thought of gifts to get for everyone in London. She planned to leave the same day Auntie Ruth and her family would leave and would be back the day they arrive.

They already booked her ride on the train for her and handed her the ticket. She went shopping to get the family and friends a few gifts. She was so happy and could not wait to be in London.

All her fears of what could happen on her way back to London, like being arrested, disappeared. Michael would pick her up at the train station.

Whilst on the train, she kept looking around as if everybody on the train or coming on the train were looking for her. She blocked her ears with her earpiece, listening to music. This helped to calm her down. Michael had called to know how the journey progressed. She could hear his excitement; she was also looking forward to seeing him.

After a ride that seemed like a long time, the train eventually arrived in London. Michael could not hide his emotions when he sighted her walking down the sidewalk. He walked to meet up with her and hugged her so tight.

"Michael, you're suffocating meeee," she said to Michael, amidst giggles.

"I'm sorry, Eva. You know I'm so happy to finally see you."

It was a pleasant ride home. They tried to catch up as much as was possible. She had an even more rousing reception when she got to her family's house. The children hugged her so much and refused to let go. Everyone was so happy to see her. They invited Michael to have dinner with them, to which he excitedly obliged.

As they ate, the children could not stop talking, telling her how much they missed her, all that had happened in their school the whole time she was away, and their new teachers and new friends.

The parents tried to shut them up, but they wouldn't stop. Michael was enjoying the entire company. He was happy to be accepted into the family. After dinner, Auntie Tonia and her husband asked to speak with him alone. Eva knew the moment of questioning had come for Michael, but she was calm and didn't entertain any worry. She had grown to love him more and would like her family to know more about him too. She left them alone and went with the children for some chitchat with Sister Bose.

"Tell us all about the new city." Sister Bose said.

"Yes, auntie Eva. What does it feel like living there?" Tobi added

"Did you make lots of friends?" Dumininu was curious. She would not be left out of the quizzing.

She settled in a raffia chair in the kitchen and told them all they wanted to know. A few hours later, her auntie called her in to join them in the sitting room. They had finished with Michael and wanted to speak with them together. Eva already sensed this would happen.

The questioning ended in a few minutes and the entire family sat to watch a movie, which finished late. Michael announced his leave and promised to visit again. He told Eva he would pick her tomorrow for a visit to Bisi's. It was going to be a surprise because she didn't know she was coming to town.

Chapter Twenty-two

She slept like a baby that night. She was exhausted from the trip and felt safe in this house that had truly become home to her. Although she knew London was not the city to be safe but right in this house, she felt safe and comfortable. She promised herself to enjoy the peace for the one week she stayed. God had been her keeper the whole time, and she knew He was not about to leave her.

The next morning, she got dressed and waited for Michael. They both promised to drop the children in school before leaving for Bisi's place. She knocked on Bisi's door.

"Whatttttt? Oh my God!!!" hugging her and excitedly shouting. "Why didn't you tell me you were coming?"

"I'm not sure I would have received this warm audience. At least now I know someone missed me."

They both laughed heartily at Eva's jokes. They had truly missed each other.

She asked them in and made them some food. She was also meeting Michael for the first time, so she was trying to make a good impression. They chatted and watched movies together. Michael took his leave so he could give them time to talk and spend together. He would pick Eva up later.

They had so much to talk about. Though they always spoke over the phone, it felt like they had not talked to each other in a long time.

"I'm going back on Friday and have a few places to visit before I leave," Eva said to Bisi.

"Can we have a double date one of these days so I can introduce you to my man?" Bisi requested.

Eva felt it was a good idea and promised to ask Michael when he would be free.

Michael picked her up later, and they went for a drink. He could have some time alone with her. He told her he had mentioned her to his family too and hoped that she would meet them soon.

The week went by so fast that she didn't feel like going back to Manchester, but she knew she had to.

It had been a lovely week, meeting up with friends and spending time with her family. Michael decided to drive her back, even though Eva remembered Bisi saying she should be careful when she was in someone's car because the police could stop them, ask for their papers, and arrest, detain, and deport her. But right now, she was too happy to think about that.

If she had to follow all the dos and don'ts, she would not even go out. The rules were a lot to abide by. Don't talk to people, don't have friends, only take public transport, etc.

Living without your voice was the hardest way to live one's life, but she was ready to risk it this one time by allowing Michael to drive her to Manchester. She had enjoyed their time together and was looking to spend more time with him. This one week had drawn them closer, and they didn't want to part, though they knew they had to. Michael would drop her at Manchester and stay in an hotel for the night.

They had a lot to talk about through the journey, including plans to always visit regularly. By the time they got to Manchester, Auntie Ruth had called that they were back at home. Michael dropped her straight at home and left for his hotel. It was hard for them to part but they had to.

Chapter Twenty-three

She returned to her life in Manchester. Years went by with no difference or hopes of getting her settlement papers. In the meantime, she completed her studies online while doing some other small courses. Meanwhile, Michael completed his Medical studies and sent Eva an invite to his graduation. She was excited about it, yet skeptical about going as she would meet Michael's family for the first time.

A small reception was organised for the evening after the graduation ceremony. Bisi and Sophie had helped her with her choice of what to wear. It was a lovely red dress. They were particular about Eva's look since she would meet her future parents-in-law. Eva had to playfully remind them that Michael was yet to propose to her.

Bisi and Sophie could not attend the ceremony with her because she had only one invite for herself. The graduation went very well, with Michael getting four awards. His parents and his grandmother were very nice to her, treating her like they had known her for so long.

Once the ceremony was over, Michael walked straight towards her to hug her. This made her feel special, as she felt like they were the only ones in the room. The area booked for the reception was exquisite and well decorated.

While they were eating, the lights went off, leaving only the candle lights on the table. A saxophonist was heard playing. Eva was enthralled and thought it was very romantic and serene. Michael excused himself to go to the loo. Just a few seconds later, she felt a figure by her back. She was scared but tried to comport herself so she didn't look back.

What if there was no one beside her? Just then, she heard Michael's mum calling her name. She nearly jumped off her chair in fright.

As she answered, his mum asked her to please help bring the file Michael had left on the table. She stood up, moving her chair back, and right there was Michael on one knee with a ring box in his hand. Eva was shy and didn't know what to say.

She mouthed the words, "Michael, what are you doing?"

Right there, he proposed. She could hear a few familiar voices through the dimly lit room say "say yes." The voices sounded familiar, so she turned and saw Auntie Tonia and her husband, Auntie Ruth, and Uncle Niyi, Sister Bose, the children, Bisi and her fiancé, and Sophie and her boyfriend. She was shocked, as she didn't know they were all part of this.

She eventually steadied her posture and turned to Michael. He said a few words, and she said "Yes!" The lights and loud music eventually came back on. The ring was so beautiful. The rest of the night was lovely.

After several months, they got married. With Michael and her auntie's help, her parents could attend her wedding. Immediately after their wedding, Michael was so eager to start the procedure for Eva's settlement paper. They moved back to London, into a house Michael had bought. He also got an offer from a hospital in London to work.

Eva was so happy that looking back now, she knew God had it all planned out for her. Her life has turned around for good. She was full of praises to God as she reminisced over all she went through. Life had definitely turned out great for her after 7years of losing her voice and identity. God truly had been good to her.